BY DAN SIMMONS

THE HYPERION CANTOS
Hyperion
The Fall of Hyperion
Endymion
The Rise of Endymion

ILIUM/OLYMPOS CYCLE
Ilium
Olympos

JOE KURTZ NOVELS
Hardcase
Hard Freeze
Hard as Nails

SUMMER OF NIGHT SERIES
Summer of Night
Children of the Night
Fires of Eden
A Winter Haunting

OTHER NOVELS
Song of Kali
Carrion Comfort
Phases of Gravity
Entropy's Bed at Midnight
The Hollow Man
The Crook Factory
The Terror
Drood
Black Hills
Flashback
The Abominable
The Fifth Heart

HYPERION

HYPERION

DAN SIMMONS

DEL REY

2017 Del Rey Trade Paperback Edition

Published in the United States by Del Rey, an imprint of Random House, a division of Penguin Random House LLC, New York.

DEL REY and the HOUSE colophon are registered trademarks of Penguin Random House LLC.

Originally published in the United States in hardcover by Doubleday, an imprint of the Knopf Doubleday Publishing Group, a division of Penguin Random House LLC, in 1989.

ISBN 978-0-399-17861-0
Ebook ISBN 978-0-307-78188-8

Printed in the United States on acid-free paper.

randomhousebooks.com

12 14 16 18 19 17 15 13

Book design by Diane Hobbing

This is for Ted

HYPERION